Call of the Wild

*Retold from the Jack London
original by Oliver Ho*

Illustrated by Lucy Corvino

STERLING

New York / London
www.sterlingpublishing.com/kids

STERLING and the distinctive Sterling logo are registered trademarks of
Sterling Publishing Co., Inc.

Library of Congress Cataloging-in-Publication Data

Ho, Oliver.
  The call of the wild / abridged by Oliver Ho; illustrated by Lucy Corvino;
retold from the Jack London original.
      p. cm.—(Classic starts)
  Summary: An abridged version of the tale of an unusual dog, part St.
Bernard, part Scotch shepherd, that is forcibly taken to the Klondike gold
fields where he eventually becomes the leader of a wolf pack.
  ISBN 1-4027-1274-X
  1. Dogs—Juvenile fiction. [1. Dogs—Fiction. 2. Wolves—Fiction. 3. Yukon
Territory—Fiction. 4. Canada—History—1867–1914—Fiction.] I. Corvino,
Lucy, ill. II. London, Jack, 1876–1916. Call of the wild. III. Title. IV. Series.
PZ10.3.H643 Cal 2004
[Fic]—dc22

                                                    2004013645

                              8 10 9 7

Published by Sterling Publishing Co., Inc.
387 Park Avenue South, New York, NY 10016
Copyright © 2005 by Oliver Ho
Illustrations copyright © 2005 by Lucy Corvino
Distributed in Canada by Sterling Publishing
c/o Canadian Manda Group, 165 Dufferin Street
Toronto, Ontario, Canada M6K 3H6
Distributed in the United Kingdom by GMC Distribution Services,
Castle Place, 166 High Street, Lewes, East Sussex, England BN7 1XU
Distributed in Australia by Capricorn Link (Australia) Pty. Ltd.
P.O. Box 704, Windsor, NSW 2756, Australia

Classic Starts is a trademark of Sterling Publishing Co., Inc.

Printed in China
All Rights Reserved
Design by Renato Stanisic

Sterling ISBN 978-1-4027-1274-6

For information about custom editions, special sales, premium and
corporate purchases, please contact Sterling Special Sales
Department at 800-805-5489 or specialsales@sterlingpublishing.com.

CONTENTS

CHAPTER 1

Kidnapped

B uck did not read the newspapers. If he did, he would have known that trouble was brewing, not only for himself, but for every dog, strong of muscle and with warm, long hair, from Puget Sound to San Diego. A little while ago, some men, who lived far north in the Arctic darkness, had found a yellow metal that was worth a lot of money. Now, thousands of men were heading north in pursuit of that metal they called gold. These men wanted dogs, and the dogs they wanted were dogs like Buck, heavy dogs with strong muscles and furry coats to protect them from the cold.

Buck lived at a big house in the sun-kissed Santa Clara Valley in California. Judge Miller's place, as it was called, stood back from the road, half hidden among the trees, through which glimpses could be caught of the wide porch that ran around its four sides. The house was approached by gravel driveways, which wound about through wide lawns. Behind the house were great stables, where a dozen grooms and boys worked, rows of vine-clad servants' cottages, long grapevines, green pastures, orchards, and berry patches. There was a large well, and the big cement tank where Judge Miller's boys took their morning swim and kept cool in the hot afternoon.

And over this great estate Buck ruled. Here he was born, and here he had lived the four years of his life. It was true, there were other dogs, there could not but be other dogs on so vast a place, but they did not count. They came and went, resided in the populous kennels, or lived quietly in the corners of the house like Toots, the Japanese pug, or Ysabel, the Mexican hairless—strange creatures that rarely put nose out of doors or set foot to ground. On the other hand, there were the fox terriers, a score of them at least, who yelped fearful promises at Toots and Ysabel looking out of the windows at them and protected by a legion of housemaids armed with brooms and mops.

But Buck was not a house dog or a kennel dog. He looked after the entire place. He plunged into the swimming tank or went hunting with the Judge's sons; he escorted Mollie and Alice, the Judge's daughters, on long twilight or early-morning walks around the estate; on wintry nights he lay at the Judge's feet before the roaring library fire. He carried the Judge's grandsons on his back, rolled them in the grass, and guarded their footsteps through wild adventures down to the fountain in the stable yard, and even beyond, where the horse stables stood, and the berry patches grew. He walked like a king past the kennel dogs and utterly ignored Toots and Ysabel because he was king—king over all creeping, crawling, flying things of Judge Miller's place, humans included.

Buck's father, Elmo, a huge St. Bernard, had been the Judge's close friend, and Buck tried to follow in the way of his father. He was not so large—he weighed only one hundred and forty pounds—for his mother, Shep, had been a smaller Scotch shepherd dog. Still, one hundred and forty pounds, to which was added the dignity that comes of good living and universal respect, enabled him to carry himself in right royal fashion. During the four years since his puppyhood, he had a fine pride in himself, and was even a trifle bit arrogant, as country gentlemen can sometimes become. But he had saved himself by not becoming a mere pampered house dog. Hunting and running outdoors had kept down the fat and hardened his muscles. He also loved to play and swim.

This was the kind of dog Buck was in the fall of 1897, when the Klondike gold rush dragged men from all over the world into the frozen North. But Buck did not read the newspapers, and he did not know that Manuel, one of the gardeners, had one dangerous problem: he loved to gamble.

One night when the Judge was at a meeting, and the boys were busy—on the memorable night of Manuel's treachery—no one saw him and Buck go off through the orchard on what Buck imagined was just a stroll. And except for one other man, no one saw them arrive at the tiny trail station known as College Park. This man talked with Manuel, and gave him money.

"You might wrap up the goods before you

deliver them," the stranger said gruffly, and Manuel looped a piece of strong rope around Buck's neck under the collar.

"Twist it, an' you'll choke 'm plenty," said Manuel, and the stranger nodded his head.

Buck accepted the rope with quiet dignity. To be sure, he didn't like it, but he had learned to trust in men he knew, and to give them credit for knowing more than he did. But when the ends of the rope were placed in the stranger's hands, which pulled him, Buck growled angrily. To his surprise the rope tightened around his neck, making it hard to breathe. Never in all his life had he been so vilely treated, and never in all his life had he been so angry. But he could not escape. Soon after, a train stopped and the two men threw him into the baggage car.

The next he knew, he was dimly aware that his tongue hurt and that he was being jolted along in some kind of vehicle. The hoarse shriek of a train whistle told him where he was. He had traveled too often with the Judge not to know how it felt to ride in a baggage car. He opened his eyes and felt as angry as a kidnapped king. He saw in front of him the man who had taken him and he began barking wildly at the man and even managed to bite one of the man's hands.

Buck's barking made so much noise that one of the baggage men came in to see what was going on. Seeing that the man who had taken Buck had been bitten, he asked if there was something wrong with the dog. "Yep, this dog has fits," the man lied. "I'm takin' him up for his owner to San Francisco. A crack dog doctor up there thinks that he can cure him."

After the train finally reached San Francisco, the man took Buck to a little shed in back of a saloon near the waterfront.

"All I get is fifty for this," the man grumbled to the saloon keeper. Pointing to his sore hand, the man continued, "an' I wouldn't do it over for a thousand, cold cash. That dog is as fierce as they come."

"Stop your complaining," the saloon keeper said. "You got the money we agreed on and not a penny more or a penny less, didn't you? Besides, where this dog is going, you won't meet up with him again. That I can promise."

"I sure hope so," the other man muttered and rubbed his sore hand again. "I'll not soon forget the likes of this one, that's for sure."

Tired as he was, Buck still tried to fight, but finally he was thrown down and held by a group of men who took the heavy brass collar off his neck. Then they took off the rope from his neck and shoved Buck into a wooden crate that was like a cage.

There Buck stayed for the rest of the night. He could not understand what it all meant. What did they want with him, these strange men? Why were they keeping him in this narrow crate? He did not know why, but he also felt more trouble coming.

Several times during the night Buck sprang to his feet when the shed door rattled open, hoping to see the Judge, or the boys at least. But each time he only saw the big face of the saloon keeper, who looked in at him by the light of a candle. And each time the joyful bark that grew in Buck's throat was changed into a savage growl.

But the saloon keeper let him alone, and in the morning four new men entered and picked up the crate. More bad men, Buck decided, for they were evil-looking creatures, ragged and dirty; and he barked and growled at them as best he could. They only laughed and poked sticks at him, which he grabbed with his teeth till he realized that they wanted to anger him. Now Buck lay down and allowed the crate to be lifted into a wagon. Then he, and the crate in which he was held, began another long journey. After a wagon ride, he was placed, along with a bunch of boxes and parcels, onto a ferryboat. After that, a truck took him to a big train station, and finally, he was put in an express train car. Buck didn't know was next for him but he couldn't help feeling that he wouldn't see his old home for a long time to come.

For two days and nights this express car traveled; and for two days and nights Buck did not eat or drink. In his rage he had barked and growled at everyone he saw. Sometimes after he threw himself against the bars in anger, a few people would laugh and tease him. They growled and barked back at him pretending to be dogs, or they meowed like cats, or flapped their arms like birds. It was all very silly, he knew; but still his anger grew and grew. He did not mind the not being fed so much, but the lack of water made his tongue and throat feel dry and swollen.

He was glad for one thing: the rope was finally off his neck, and he made up his mind that they would never put another rope on him again. His eyes turned red, and he was now so angry that the Judge himself would not have recognized him. Everyone who saw Buck on the train was very happy when the crate that carried Buck was finally unloaded at Seattle.

Four men gingerly carried the crate from the wagon into a small backyard with high walls around it. A stout man wearing a red sweater came out and signed the receipt book for the driver. The driver also gave the man a letter from the saloon keeper in San Francisco that the man in the red sweater carefully read. That must be the man, Buck figured, who would be his next tormentor, and he hurled himself savagely against the bars. The man smiled grimly, and brought a hatchet and a club.

"You ain't going to take him out now?" the driver asked.

"Sure," the man replied, driving the hatchet into the crate.

The four men who had carried the crate in ran to a safe space on the top of the wall just in case Buck escaped.

At the first sound of the crate being opened, Buck rushed forward, sinking his teeth into the splinters of wood and pulling at them. Snarling and growling, Buck was as anxious to get out as the man in the red sweater was intent on getting him out.

"Now, you red-eyed devil," the man said, when he had made an opening large enough for Buck to get through. At the same time he dropped the hatchet and shifted the club to his right hand.

And Buck was truly a red-eyed devil, as he drew himself together for the spring, hair bristling, mouth foaming, a mad glitter in his bloodshot eyes. He threw his one hundred and forty pounds of fury right at the man with all the pent-up rage that had been building up inside him after two full days and nights without any food or water. In midair, just as he was about to bite the man, he received a shock that stopped his body. He spun over, hitting the ground on his back and side.

Buck had never been struck by a club in his life, and did not understand what had just happened. With a snarl that was part bark and more scream he was again on his feet and launched into the air. And again the shock came and he again fell to the ground.

"He's no slouch at dog breakin', that's what I say," one of the men on the wall cried happily.

"The dog's name is Buck," the man in the red

sweater replied, as he gently patted Buck on the top of his head. "That's what the letter from the saloon keeper in San Francisco said."

Then turning to the still-dazed dog, he continued in a gentle voice, "Well, Buck, my boy, we've had our little fight, and the best thing we can do is to let it go at that. You've learned your place, and I know mine. Be a good dog and all'll go well. Be a bad dog and you will be in trouble. Understand?"

When the man then brought him water, Buck drank eagerly, and he later gobbled down a generous meal of raw meat, chunk by chunk, from the man's hand.

Even though Buck took the food and water happily, it didn't mean that he accepted what the man did to him. Buck knew that this time he had lost the fight; but he hadn't given up. He now learned, once for all, that he could not simply rely on his strength to win. In the future he knew he would also have to figure out ways to survive that didn't rely just on his muscles but on his cunning as well. That day the man in the red sweater had taught him a lesson he would never forget.

CHAPTER 2

Snow

As the days went by, other dogs came, in crates and at the ends of ropes, some quietly, and some barking and growling as he had come; and, one and all, he watched them accept the rule of the man in the red sweater.

Now and again other men—strangers— came into the place where Buck and the other dogs were being held. They talked excitedly to the man in the red sweater and asked him about different dogs, how strong they were, and how much they cost. Then the strangers took one or more of the dogs away with them. Buck wondered where they went, for they never came back. He felt scared not knowing what happened to the dogs after they left, and he was glad each time when he was not sold.

Then one day Buck was chosen by a small man named Perrault. Perrault worked for the Canadian government. His job was to deliver mail in the Arctic North, and he knew the kind of dog he needed for the job and would pay well for it. Perrault was excited when he saw Buck, and he asked the man in the red sweater how much he would cost.

"Three hundred, and that's a special price for you, Perrault, you being a good customer and all," said the man in the red sweater. Then with a smile he continued, "I've been saving this one especially for you. His name is Buck and he's a fierce one all right. Just the kind of dog you need to get the job done."

Perrault grinned. Considering that the price of dogs had gone up so much recently because of the gold rush, it was a fair price for such a fine dog. With his long experience, Perrault knew dogs like an expert, and when he looked at Buck he could tell that he was one in a thousand—"Or maybe one in ten thousand," he said quietly.

Buck saw Perrault give money to the man in the red sweater. Then Buck and another dog named Curly, a good-natured Newfoundland, were led away by Perrault. Curly and Buck left Seattle on a ship called the *Narwhal*. They were taken below by Perrault and given to a large man named François. These men were new to Buck, and even though he did not like them, he was able to respect them. He learned that Perrault and François were fair and calm and that both men knew a great deal about how to handle dogs.

Between decks on the *Narwhal*, Buck and Curly met two other dogs. One of them was a big, snow-white dog. He seemed friendly, but he had a way of smiling that meant he was really thinking up some mean trick. Once, he even stole from Buck's food. As Buck chased him, François got the food away from the dog first, and gave it back to Buck.

The other dog Buck and Curly met wanted to be left alone. Dave was his name, and he just ate and slept, or yawned between times and took an interest in nothing, not even when the *Narwhal* crossed rough waters and rolled from side to side. When Buck and Curly got excited and scared, Dave only raised his head. He looked like he was annoyed. He glanced at Buck and Curly, yawned, and went to sleep again.

Many days and nights passed, and Buck noticed the weather was growing colder each day. One morning, the ship was quiet, and all the dogs became excited. They all knew a change was coming. François put them all on leashes and brought them on deck. At his first step on the cold ground,

Buck's feet sank into white mushy stuff, very much like mud. He jumped back with a snort. More of this white stuff was falling through the air. He shook himself, but more of it fell on him. He sniffed it curiously, and then licked some up on his tongue. It burned his tongue a little bit, and in the next instant it was gone. This puzzled him. He tried it again, with the same results. The other dogs and people who watched this laughed at him, and he felt embarrassed. But he did not know why. It was the first time he had ever seen snow.

The snow was not all that Buck had to master. Buck's first day on Dyea Beach was a nightmare. There was a new shock and surprise every hour. He felt like he had been taken from a civilized society and thrown into a primitive world. Here there was no sun-filled, lazy life, like the one he had at Judge

Miller's place, with nothing to do but loaf around and be bored. Here there was no peace, no rest—not a moment's safety. All around him was confusion and action, and at every moment there was danger. He had to be alert all the time. These dogs and men were not like the ones he had known in the past. These were dangerous, and the only law they knew was the law of rope and fang.

He had never seen dogs fight like this, and his first experience taught him an unforgettable lesson. While they were camped near the log store, Curly, in her friendly way, approached a husky dog. He was the size of a full-grown wolf, but not half as large as she. Without warning, the husky jumped and knocked her down.

It was the wolf style of fighting to jump in, strike, and jump away. But there was more to it than this. Thirty or forty huskies ran to the spot and surrounded the two dogs in a silent, threatening circle. Buck did not understand why. Curly tried to fight the other dog, but he knocked her down again. Then the other dogs closed in around her. They were barking, biting, and scaring her.

This happened so suddenly, and was so unexpected, that Buck did not know what to do. He saw a dog named Spitz stick his tongue out in the strange way he had of laughing. Buck also saw François swinging a stick and running into the group of dogs to chase them away. Three other men were helping him to scatter them. It did not take long, but Curly was hurt, and François took her away. It had not been fair, Buck thought. So that was the way of these dogs, was it? Once down, they were all over you. Well, he would see to it that he never went down. Spitz stuck his tongue out and laughed again, and from that moment Buck disliked him more than any dog or man he had ever met.

Before he had recovered from the shock of seeing what had happened to Curly, Buck received another shock. François attached an arrangement of straps and buckles to him. It was a harness, like the ones he had seen people put on the horses at home. And the same way he had seen the horses work, so was Buck put to work, hauling François on a sled to the forest that was at the edge of the valley, and returning with a load of firewood. Buck did not like the work, but he was too wise to fight back. He buckled down with all his strength and did his best, even though it was all new and strange. François was stern with the dogs, and Spitz was their leader. He and Dave were the most experienced dogs, and they taught Buck by snapping and barking at him when he made mistakes. Buck learned quickly from the two dogs and François. Before they returned to camp, Buck knew to stop at "Ho," to go ahead at "Mush," to swing wide on the bends, and to keep clear of the other dogs when the loaded sled shot downhill at their heels.

"Three very good dogs," François told Perrault. "That Buck, he pulls like mad. I'll be able to teach him quick as anything."

By afternoon, Perrault, who was in a hurry to be on the trail with his mail delivery, returned with two more dogs. Billee and Joe, he called them, two brothers, and both true huskies. Even though they had the same mother, the brothers were as different as night and day. Billee was good-natured, while Joe was the opposite—sour and brooding, with a constant snarl and a mean look. Buck welcomed them, Dave ignored them, and Spitz bullied them. Billee wagged his tail at first, and then ran away when he saw that Spitz was mean. But no matter how Spitz tried, Joe stood face-to-face with him even though he was terrified. Joe's mane bristled, his ears laid back, and he was snarling. He looked so mean and scared that Spitz finally gave up, but to make up for it, he continued to chase Billee.

By evening, Perrault added another dog to the group. This one was an old husky—long, lean, and gaunt, with a battle-scarred face and a single eye. He was called Sol-leks, which means "the Angry One." Like Dave, he asked nothing, gave nothing, and expected nothing. And when he marched slowly into their group, even Spitz left him alone. He had one habit that Buck was unlucky enough to discover. Sol-leks did not like to be approached on his blind side. Buck did this by mistake and Sol-leks whirled and barked at him. Forever afterward Buck avoided his blind side, and never had any trouble with him again. It seemed as if his only ambition, like Dave's, was to be left alone.

CHAPTER 3

Learning to Survive

⟡

That night, Buck faced the great problem of sleeping. The tent, lit by a candle, glowed warmly. Everything around them was white and snowy. When Buck entered the tent, thinking it was a normal thing to do, Perrault and François yelled at him and threw things at him until he ran away, angry and embarrassed, back into the cold. A chill wind was blowing that nipped him sharply. He lay down on the snow and tried to sleep, but the frost soon drove him shivering to his feet. Miserable, he wandered around among the many tents, only to find that one place was just as cold as another. Here and there, rude dogs tried to bully him, but he bristled his neck hair and snarled (for he was learning fast how to fight back), and they let him go on his way without bothering him anymore.

Finally, an idea came to him. He would return and see how his own teammates were sleeping. To his surprise, they had disappeared. Again he wandered around the large camp, looking for them, and again he returned without finding them. Were they in the tent? No, that could not be, or else he would not have been chased out. Then where could they possibly be? With drooping tail and shivering body, feeling very lost and alone, he circled the tent. Suddenly the snow gave way under his front legs and he sank down. Something wriggled under his feet. He sprang back, bristling and snarling, afraid of the unknown. But a friendly little yelp reassured him, and he went back to investigate. He smelled a whiff of warm air, and there, curled up under the snow in a snug ball, lay Billee. He whined, squirmed, and wriggled to show that he was friendly, and even licked Buck's face with his warm wet tongue.

Another lesson. So that was the way they did it. Buck chose a spot and, with much fuss and hard work, dug a hole for himself. Soon, the heat from

his body filled the small space and he was asleep. The day had been long and hard, and he slept soundly and comfortably, even though he growled and barked and wrestled with bad dreams.

He did not open his eyes until the noises of the camp woke him. At first, he did not know where he was. It had snowed during the night and he was completely buried. The snow walls pressed in on him from every side, and he felt very scared. His muscles tensed and the hair on his neck and shoulders stood on end. With a ferocious snarl, he jumped straight up into the blinding day, the snow flying about him in a flashing cloud. Before he landed on his feet, he saw the white camp around him and knew where he was. Buck then remembered all that had happened from the time he went for a stroll with Manuel to the hole he had dug for himself the night before.

François shouted when he saw Buck.

"What did I say?" he yelled to Perrault. "That Buck for sure learns quick as anything."

Perrault nodded, with a serious look on his face. As a courier for the Canadian government, carrying important mail, he wanted to get the best dogs, and he was happy that he had found Buck.

Three more huskies were added to the team in less than an hour, making a total of nine, and in fifteen minutes they were all in harness and swinging up the trail toward the Dyea Canyon. Buck was glad to be gone, and even though the work was hard, he found that he did not mind it. He was surprised at the team's eagerness, and even more surprised at the change that had come over Dave and Sol-leks. They were like new dogs, completely altered by the harness. They were not quiet and solitary anymore. They were alert and active, anxious that the work should go well, and angry with anything that slowed their work. The hard work seemed to be the only thing that made them happy.

Dave was the wheeler, or sled dog. Pulling in front of him was Buck; then came Sol-leks. The rest of the team was ahead of them in single file all the way to the leader, who was Spitz.

Buck had been placed between Dave and Sol-leks so he could learn from the two older dogs. Buck was a good student, and they were good teachers, never letting Buck make a mistake for long. Dave was fair and very wise. Once, during a brief stop, Buck got tangled in the ropes and delayed the start. Dave and Sol-leks became very angry with him, and Buck took care to keep clear of the ropes afterward. Before the day was over, he had done so well that Dave and Sol-leks stopped bothering him about it. Perrault even honored him by lifting Buck's feet and carefully examining them.

It was a hard day's run, up the canyon, through Sheep Camp, past the Scales and the tree line, across glaciers and snowdrifts hundreds of feet deep, and over the great Chilcoot Divide, which stands between the saltwater and the freshwater and guards the sad and lonely North. They made good time down the chain of lakes that fill the craters of extinct volcanoes. Late that night they pulled into the huge camp at Lake Bennett, where thousands of gold seekers were building boats and waiting for the ice to break up in the spring. Buck made his hole in the snow and slept well, but he was woken up much too soon in the cold darkness and harnessed with the other dogs to the sled.

That day they were able to run forty miles because the snow on the trail was packed, which made the traveling easier. But the next day, and for many to follow, they had to break their own trail in fresh snow. This meant that they had to work harder, and traveled slower. Perrault traveled ahead of the team, packing the snow with his snowshoes to make it easier for them. François guided the sled and sometimes changed places with him, but not often. Perrault was in a hurry, and he took pride in his knowledge of snow and ice. It was important to know about ice because they had to travel across it for months at a time. In the fall, the ice was very thin, and where there was fast-running water, there was no ice at all.

Day after day, Buck worked hard. They always stopped and made camp in the dark, eating their bit of fish, and crawling to sleep in the snow; by the time the sun rose, they were already many miles onto the trail again. Buck was very hungry. The pound and a half of dried salmon, which was his food for the day, seemed to go nowhere. He never had enough. The other dogs, because they weighed less and were used to this way of life, received only a pound of fish to eat, and managed to stay in good shape.

Buck quickly lost the neatness that was such an important part of his old life. He used to be a careful eater, but he found that the other dogs, finishing first, would steal his food. There was no way to defend it. While he was chasing away two or three, others would eat his food. So he ate as fast as they did. And he was often so hungry that he would steal food from any dogs that ate slower. He watched and learned. When he saw Pike, one of the new dogs, who was a clever thief, steal a slice of bacon when Perrault's back was turned, Buck did the same thing the next day, and got away with the whole chunk. Perrault was very angry, but did not suspect Buck, while Dub, an awkward dog who was always getting caught, was punished for it.

This first theft made Buck able to survive in

the North. It showed that he could adapt, which was very important. It also showed that he didn't care anymore about stealing. There was no other choice for Buck in this cold and difficult place. He did not steal because he liked to do it, but because he was hungry. And he stole things carefully and secretly, because he did not want to be punished.

He changed quickly. His muscles became hard as iron, and he was able to ignore ordinary pain. He could eat anything. His body would turn any food into energy to toughen and strengthen his muscles.

His senses of sight and scent became very keen, and his hearing became so sharp that in his sleep he could hear the quietest sound and know exactly what it was. He learned to bite the ice out with his teeth when it collected between his toes. When he was thirsty, if there was a layer of ice over the water hole, he would break it by standing on his hind legs and then coming down and smashing the ice with his front legs. He could even predict the weather just by smelling the air.

Buck did not learn only by experience. Instincts he did not even know he had became active in him. He felt like he could remember when wild dogs ran in packs through the forest and hunted their own food. When he fought with the other dogs, he felt like one of his ancestors fighting. This old kind of life and its tricks came to him without trying, as if they had always been his. And when, on cold nights, he pointed his nose at a star and howled long, like a wolf, it felt like one of his ancestors was howling through the centuries, and through him. His voice was their voice.

Buck's life had changed so much, all because some men had found a yellow metal in the North, and because Manuel was a gardener's helper who loved to gamble.

CHAPTER 4

The Strongest Dog

⌒

There was a desire in Buck to be the strongest dog in the group, and under the hard conditions of trail life, that part of him grew and grew. But he kept it a secret. He had a sense of sneakiness and cunning that was new to him, and it helped him appear calm and in control. He was too busy adjusting to his new life to feel comfortable. He never picked fights with any of the dogs, and avoided fighting whenever he could. Even though he and Spitz did not like each other, and that dislike grew every day, Buck did not let it show.

On the other hand, possibly because he sensed that Buck could take his place as leader of the pack, Spitz never let a chance pass to show his teeth. He went out of his way to bully Buck, and he always tried to start a fight that could only end with one of them running away.

This almost happened early in the trip, but an accident got in the way. At the end of this day, they had made camp on the shore of Lake Le Barge. It was bleak and miserable. Driving snow, a wind that was sharp as a knife, and total darkness forced them to search blindly for a camping place. They could not have chosen worse. At their backs there was a wall of rock, and Perrault and François had to make their fire and spread their sleeping bags on the ice of the lake itself. They had thrown the tent away so they could travel light. They used a few sticks of driftwood to make their fire, but it burned through the ice and left them to eat supper in the dark.

Close to the wall of rock, Buck had dug his hole in the snow. He was so snug and warm in it that he did not want to leave when François gave out the fish, after thawing it over the fire. When Buck finished eating and returned to his hole, he found another dog in it. A warning snarl told him it was Spitz. Until then, Buck had avoided trouble with his enemy, but this was too much. The beast in him roared. He sprang on Spitz with a fury that surprised them both. Spitz was especially surprised because his whole experience with Buck had told him that Buck was usually a timid and quiet dog who managed to hold his own with the other dogs only because of his great weight and size.

François was surprised, too, when they rolled out in a tangle from the sleeping hole, and he guessed why they were fighting.

"A-a-ah!" he cried to Buck. "Give it to him, by God! Give it to him, the dirty thief!"

Spitz was just as willing to fight. He was crying with anger and eagerness as he circled back and forth, looking for a moment to jump in. Buck was also eager, but just as careful, as he circled back and forth. It was then that something unexpected happened that made them wait for another time to fight.

Perrault yelled, and there was the sound of barking. The camp was suddenly alive with other animals. They were starving wild huskies, four or five dozen of them, who had smelled the camp from a nearby village. They had crept in while Buck and Spitz were fighting, and when the two men jumped in among the wild dogs, they showed their teeth and fought back. The smell of food made them crazy. Perrault found one eating from the grub box, where the men stored all the food. He chased that one away, but the grub box was knocked over, and right away more of the wild dogs were scrambling for the bread and bacon. They yelped and howled as the men tried to scare them away.

In the meantime, the astonished sled dogs had burst out of their sleeping holes only to be jumped on by the fierce invaders. Buck had never seen such dogs. They were so skinny it seemed as though he could see their skeletons through their skin. Their eyes were blazing and they showed their teeth. Their hunger made them very scary, and it was impossible to fight them off. The sled dogs were pushed back against the cliff during the first attack. Three huskies tried to fight with Buck. The sound was very frightening. Billee was crying. Dave and Sol-leks were fighting bravely side by side. Joe was barking like a monster. Pike was running around from dog to dog. The fight was making Buck crazy and excited. It made him fierce. He chased away one dog, then felt another next to him. It was Spitz, unfairly attacking him again from the side.

Perrault and François chased away the wild dogs from their part of the camp and then hurried to help their sled dogs. The starving dogs moved away, and Buck shook himself free. But it was only for a moment. The two men had to run back to save the grub, where the wild dogs had run. When the men chased them away, the huskies returned to attack the team. Billee, terrified into bravery, sprang through the savage circle of wild dogs and ran away over the ice. Pike and Dub followed, with the rest of the team behind them. As Buck got ready to spring after them, out of the corner of his eye he saw Spitz rush at him, to try to knock him over. He managed to get out of the way and join the other sled dogs running across the frozen lake.

Later, the nine sled dogs gathered together and looked for shelter in the forest. They were not being chased anymore, but they felt very bad. They were all tired and hurt from the fight. At daybreak they limped back to camp to find the invaders gone and the two men in angry moods. Half of their food supply was gone. The huskies had chewed through the sled harness and the canvas that covered the sled. Nothing, no matter how difficult it would be to eat, had escaped them. They had eaten a pair of Perrault's moccasins, and even two feet from the end of François's whip. He was looking at it sadly when the sled dogs arrived.

"Ah, my friends," he said, softly. "Are you hurt? Maybe they've been too hurt to continue so soon, hey Perrault?"

The courier shook his head. With four hundred miles of trail still between them and Dawson, he could not afford to wait. Two hours of angry words and hard work got the harness into shape, and the wounded team was under way, struggling painfully over the hardest part of the trail. They had never been on such a difficult trail, the hardest part of the trip to Dawson.

The Thirty Mile River was wide open. Its wild water would not freeze, and it was only in the shallow parts at the edges and in the quiet places where the ice held at all. The team needed six days of exhausting work to cover those terrible thirty miles. Every step was dangerous to the dogs and men. A dozen times, Perrault, leading the way on foot, broke through the ice. He was saved each time by the long pole he carried, which he held so it would fall across the hole made by his body. But the weather was getting colder and colder, and each time he broke through the ice he had to build a fire to dry himself or else he would freeze to death.

Nothing scared Perrault off. That was why he had been chosen to be a government courier. He took all kinds of risks, always pushing forward in the frost and struggling on from dawn to dark. He hurried the team over the thin parts of the ice.

Once, the sled broke through the ice, and Dave and Buck fell in the water. They were freezing when the men dragged them out of the water. The men built a fire to warm them. The dogs were covered with ice, and the two men made them run around the fire, sweating and thawing, so close to the fire that their fur was singed by the flames.

Another time, Spitz went through the ice, dragging the whole team after him up to Buck. Buck strained backward with all his strength, his forepaws on the slippery edge and the ice shaking and snapping all around. But behind him was Dave, also straining backward, and behind the sled was François, pulling with all his might.

Perrault managed to climb a rock cliff, and, using every bit of the harness and rope woven together, the men managed to pull the dogs from the water. At the end of the day, they had only managed to travel a quarter of a mile.

By the time they made it to a river called the
Hootalinqua, where there was good ice, Buck was
exhausted. The rest of the dogs felt the same. But
Perrault, to make up for lost time, made the team
start earlier and run later than they had before.
The first day they covered thirty-five miles to the
Big Salmon River. The next day they ran thirty-
five more to the Little Salmon River. The
third day they made forty miles,

which brought them close to a place called the Five Fingers.

Buck's feet were not as hard as the other dogs' feet. His were soft from his easy life at Judge Miller's place. All day now he limped, and once camp was made, he lay down like he was asleep. Hungry as he was, he could not move to get his ration of fish, which François had to bring to him. François also rubbed Buck's feet for half an hour each night after supper, and cut off the tops of his own moccasins to make four small moccasins for Buck. These were a great relief. Buck even managed to make Perrault smile one morning, when François forgot the moccasins and Buck lay on his back, his four feet waving in the air, refusing to move without them. Later in the journey, his feet became hard from running on the trail, and the worn-out footgear was thrown away.

One morning as they were harnessing up,

Dolly, who had never done anything like this before, suddenly lost her temper. First she let out a long, sad howl that made every dog bristle with fear, and then she sprang straight at Buck. He had never seen a dog do this, but he knew something was wrong and ran away in a panic. Straightaway he raced, with Dolly one leap behind. He was so scared, and ran so fast, that she could not catch him. But she was so angry—for no reason at all other than that she was tired—that he could not get away. He ran past the trees on the island, crossed a small river filled with ice to another island, then to a third island, and back to the main river, which in desperation he tried to cross. François called to him from far away and Buck ran toward him, still one leap ahead of Dolly. Buck was gasping for air and putting all his faith in the man. François held a rope ready, and as Buck ran past him, he caught Dolly in the rope and carried her away.

Buck staggered over against the sled, exhausted, sobbing for breath, helpless. This was Spitz's chance. He sprang upon Buck, trying to knock him over and bite him. Then François had to pull Spitz away.

"One mean dog, that Spitz," Perrault said. "Someday he's going to get Buck."

"That Buck, he's twice as mean," François said. "I've been watching him. I know for sure, someday he's going to get mad, and then he'll chew up that Spitz and spit him out all over the snow."

CHAPTER 5

Rivals

From then on it was war between the two dogs. Spitz, as lead dog and master of the team, worried that this strange southern dog would take his place. And Buck certainly was strange to him. Spitz had known many southern dogs, and none of them had been strong in the camp or on the trail. They were all too soft. They could not take the hard work, the frost, and the starvation. Buck was different. He could match the huskies in strength, savagery, and cunning. He was a great dog, and what made him more dangerous was that his early experience with the man in the red sweater had taught him to save up his anger and to be patient. He was smart, and he could wait in a way that made him as sneaky as the wildest dogs.

All the dogs knew that Buck and Spitz would fight to be the leader of the team. Buck wanted it. He felt a special kind of pride, which all of the dogs that worked on the trail also felt. It was pride that made them work so hard and not want to give up. This pride changed Dave and Sol-leks every morning from mean and sullen dogs into eager, ambitious ones. Pride kept them going every day. It made Spitz the leader and also made him punish any of the dogs that could not keep up or tried to get out of hard work. It was this pride that made him afraid of Buck.

Buck threatened Spitz's leadership all the time. He kept Spitz from punishing the dogs who did not work hard enough. One night there was a heavy snowfall, and in the morning Pike, who never liked to work hard, did not appear. He was hidden in his nest under a foot of snow. François called him and searched for him. Spitz was wild with anger. He raged through the camp, smelling and digging everywhere, and snarling so loudly that Pike heard and shivered in his hiding place.

But when Spitz finally found him and tried to punish him, Buck jumped in between them, knocking Spitz backward. Pike had been shaking with fear, but when he saw this happen, he became happy and jumped on Spitz. Buck no longer remembered what it meant to fight fairly, and so he also jumped on Spitz. François broke them up quickly, and while he punished Buck, Spitz punished Pike.

As they moved closer and closer to Dawson, Buck continued to come between Spitz and the other dogs. But Buck was smart about it. He waited until François was not around. Many of the other dogs also began to be unruly, except for Dave and Sol-leks. Everything was going wrong. The dogs were always fighting and getting in trouble; Buck was always the cause, and he kept François very busy. François knew that Buck and Spitz would have a terrible fight one day, and whenever he heard trouble among the dogs, he thought Buck and Spitz were at it again.

But the chance never came, and the team pulled into Dawson one dreary afternoon with the great fight still to come. Here were many men and countless dogs, and they were all hard at work. All day the dogs ran up and down the main street in long teams, pulling sleds, and at night he could hear the jingling bells on their collars as they ran. They hauled logs for cabins and firewood up to the mines. Dogs did all the work that horses did back home in the Santa Clara Valley, at Judge Miller's place. Here and there, Buck met other southern dogs, but most of them were huskies, and had been bred for this kind of work. Every night at nine, then at twelve, and again at three, they sang together. It was a weird and eerie chant, and Buck loved joining them.

With the northern lights overhead, which looked like flames, the stars twinkling, and the land frozen under the snow, this song of the huskies sounded very sad, with long cries and half sobs. It was an old song, one of the first songs that the first huskies ever sang, so many years ago. When Buck sang with them, he felt the fear and mystery of the cold and dark.

Seven days after they pulled into Dawson, they left again. This time they were on the Yukon Trail headed back to Dyea and Salt Water, which was where they had started. Perrault was carrying letters that were even more important than the ones he had brought in. He felt as proud of his work as the dogs did, and he decided they were going to make the trip in record time. He had many reasons to think they could do it. The week's rest had helped the dogs to recover, and they were filled with energy. The trail that had been so soft on the way here was now packed down hard from the teams that had come after them. The Northwest police had also agreed to leave food and supplies for the men and dogs at two or three places along the way, and now this team was traveling with a lighter load than on their way up.

They traveled fifty miles on the first day, and the second day saw them speeding up the Yukon Trail on their way to a place called Pelly. But the good run also meant a lot of trouble for François. Buck was causing problems, and the dogs were not pulling together as a team. The dogs were not afraid of Spitz anymore. Pike stole half a fish from him one night, and he gleefully ate it under Buck's protection. Another night, Dub and Joe got into a fight with Spitz, and Spitz had to give up even though they deserved to be punished. Buck never came near Spitz without snarling and bristling menacingly. In fact, Buck behaved just like a bully.

Without a clear leader, the dogs also argued with each other, and sometimes the camp was filled with barking and howling. Dave and Solleks were the only dogs who were the same as they had been before Buck started all the trouble, but the noise made the old dogs angry. François was even more angry and frustrated because he could not control the dogs. Whenever his back was turned, they were at it again. Buck would help him control the other dogs sometimes, even though François knew Buck was behind all the trouble. But Buck was too smart to be caught red-handed. He worked hard in the harness, and the work had become enjoyable for him, but it was even more fun to get the other dogs to fight and tangle everything up.

At the mouth of the Tahkeena River, one night after supper, Dub chased a snowshoe rabbit, missed catching it, and in a second the whole team was chasing with him. A hundred yards away was a camp of the Northwest police, with fifty husky dogs of their own, which all joined in the chase. The rabbit ran down the river. Buck led the pack of sixty dogs, but he could not catch up to the rabbit. Buck felt like a hunter, and he loved it. He felt more alive than he had ever felt before.

But Spitz, who was sneaky even in the middle of a chase, left the pack and took a shortcut through the woods. Buck did not know this, and as he turned a corner, the rabbit still ahead of him, he saw another figure leap from a hill nearby. It was Spitz. The rabbit got past him because Spitz's real target was Buck.

Buck did not cry out. He did not stop, either, but ran into Spitz, shoulder-to-shoulder, so hard that they both fell. They rolled over and over in the powdery snow. Spitz stood up first, quickly, almost as if he had not been knocked over.

Right away Buck knew that the time had come for their fight. As they circled each other, snarling, ears laid back, looking for an opening, this all seemed familiar to Buck. Everything was quiet in the moonlight—the snow-covered forest and ground. Nothing moved. The dogs' breath rose slowly in the frosty air. The other dogs stood in a circle around Spitz and Buck. They, too, were silent, their eyes gleaming and their breath drifting upward. To Buck it was nothing new or strange. It felt like he was supposed to be in this fight.

Spitz was a smart fighter, and he had had a lot of practice. From Spitsbergen (where he had been born), through the Arctic, and across Canada and the Barrens, he had held his own with every dog he met, and had beaten them all.

Buck tried to bite Spitz but could not catch

him. Spitz blocked him each time. Buck rushed at Spitz many times, and he tried to drive his shoulder into Spitz's shoulder and knock him over. But each time Buck tried, Spitz leaped lightly away and bit at Buck as he passed.

The fight was getting desperate, and the other dogs waited to jump on whichever dog went down first. Buck was getting tired, and Spitz started to rush at him. Once, Buck almost fell over, and the whole circle of sixty dogs moved closer, but he got up quickly, and the other dogs sat down again and waited.

Buck had something special about him, which he was beginning to figure out. He had imagination. He fought by instinct, but he could also fight with his mind. He rushed, as if trying the shoulder trick that had failed before, but at the last moment crouched down and got close to Spitz. He grabbed Spitz's front legs in his teeth and almost knocked him over. Spitz was struggling to keep up. He saw the silent circle of dogs, with gleaming eyes, closing in on him, the same way he had seen similar circles close in on other dogs in the past. Only this time, he was the one who was beaten.

Buck would not stop, and he got in position for a final rush. The circle had moved closer until he could feel the dogs' breath on his back. He could see them behind Spitz on either side, ready to jump, and watching him. Every animal stood still as if they had turned to stone. Only Spitz shook and bristled as he staggered on his sore legs. Then Buck jumped in and finally his shoulder hit against Spitz's shoulder, and knocked him over. The dogs closed in, barking loudly and biting Spitz until he had to run away over the ice and into the darkness. Buck stood and watched him run away. He was the champion now, the strongest dog. He had beaten his enemy, and he found that it felt good.

∽

"Hey, what did I say? I told you Buck was twice as mean as Spitz," François said the next morning, when he saw that Spitz was missing and Buck had wounds from the fight. He took Buck to the fire, and in its light he pointed them out.

"That Spitz, he fights hard," said Perrault, as he looked at the cuts and bite marks on Buck.

"And that Buck fights twice as hard," François answered. "And now we will make good time. No more Spitz, no more trouble. That's for sure."

While Perrault packed the camp and loaded the sled, François began harnessing the dogs. Buck walked up to the place Spitz used to have, but François brought Sol-leks there instead. François thought Sol-leks would be the best leader now because he was the most experienced. Buck jumped at Sol-leks, pushed him back, and stood in his place.

"What's this?" François cried, slapping his thighs gleefully. "Look at Buck. He chased Spitz away and now he thinks he can take Spitz's job. Go on, get out of the way!" he shouted at Buck, but the dog refused to budge.

Seeing how stubborn Buck really was only made François laugh louder. "Hey, Perrault," he said, pointing to Buck, who now sat as still as a statue. "What kind of a dog do we have here?"

"A good one," Perrault grunted.

"Well, you tell him to move, then," François said. "I don't think he wants to listen to me anymore."

"Neither do I," Perrault said with a laugh.

Finally François grew tired of waiting. He took Buck by the scruff of the neck, and even though the dog growled, François moved him to one side and put in Sol-leks as the leader. Sol-leks did not like it, and he showed that he was afraid of Buck.

François had made his decision, but when he turned his back, Buck once again chased Sol-leks from the lead position, and Sol-leks was eager to give up his place. Now François was angry.

"I'll fix you," he cried, coming back to Buck with a rope in his hand.

Buck remembered the man in the red sweater, and retreated slowly. He did not try to charge in when François put Sol-leks in the lead position. Buck circled just out of François's reach and snarled. While he circled he watched the rope so he could dodge it if François threw it. Buck was becoming wise to the way of ropes. François continued his work, and he called to Buck when he was ready to put him in his old place in front of Dave. Buck retreated two or three steps. François followed him, and Buck retreated again. After a few more tries, François threw down the rope to show Buck that he would not use it. But Buck was not going back to his old position. He wanted to be the leader. He had earned it, and he would not be happy with anything less.

Perrault joined in to help François. Between them they ran around for almost an hour. They threw ropes at Buck. He dodged. They yelled at him. He barked back and kept out of reach. He did not try to run away, but retreated around and around the camp, showing that when they would give him what he wanted, he would come in and be good.

François sat down and scratched his head. Perrault looked at his watch and was angry. Time was flying, and they should have been on the trail an hour ago. François scratched his head again. He shook it and grinned at Perrault, who shrugged his shoulders. The men were beaten. Then François went to Sol-leks and called to Buck. Buck laughed, as dogs laugh, but kept his distance. François moved Sol-leks back to his old place. Once more François called, and once more Buck laughed and kept away.

"Throw down your rope," Perrault said.

François did this, and then Buck trotted in, laughing like a champion, and took his place at the head of the team. They attached him to the harness and then broke the sled out of the ice and snow. Both men ran next to the sled as they pulled out onto the trail.

Buck now proved himself a great leader. He was even better than Spitz, whom François had thought was the best he had ever seen.

Dave and Sol-leks did not mind the change in leadership. It was none of their business. All they wanted to do was work, and work hard, in the harness. As long as no one bothered their work, they did not care what happened. The rest of the team, however, had grown unruly, and even they were surprised at how quickly Buck got them into shape.

Pike, who pulled behind Buck, and who never did more work than he had to, was quickly punished for not working hard enough. Before the day was over, he was pulling more than he had ever done in his life.

The whole team started to feel better. They worked as one unit again. At the Rink Rapids, two new huskies, Teek and Koona, were added, and Buck got them in shape so quickly that it took François's breath away.

"There's never been a dog like Buck!" he cried. "Never! He's worth a thousand dollars, hey? What do you say, Perrault?"

Perrault nodded. He was ahead of the record then, and gaining day by day. The trail was in excellent condition, and there was no fresh snow. It was not too cold. The men took turns riding in the sled and running next to it.

The Thirty Mile River was covered with ice now, and in one day they traveled the same distance it had taken them ten days to travel on their way in. In one run they made a sixty-mile dash from Lake Le Barge to the White Horse Rapids. Across the Marsh, Tagish, and Bennett Lakes, they ran so fast that the man whose turn it was to run had to hang on to a rope that was tied to the sled. On the last night of the second week, they reached White Pass and could see the lights of Skaguay in the distance.

It was a record run. Each day, for fourteen days, they had averaged forty miles. For three days after they arrived in the town of Skaguay, Perrault and François celebrated in the main street, and everyone offered to buy them food and drinks, while the dog team was the center of a crowd of admiring dog drivers.

CHAPTER 6

New Trials

⌒

After a few days, the celebrations ended, and everyone got back to business. Official orders came, calling François and Perrault to new places, and they had to leave their team. François called Buck to him, threw his arms around him, and cried over him. That was the last time Buck saw François and Perrault. Like other men, they passed out of Buck's life for good.

A Scottish man took charge of Buck and his teammates, and along with a dozen other dog teams, he started back over the trail to Dawson.

There was no light running now, no trying for a record time, only hard work each day, with a heavy load in the sled. This was the mail train that carried letters to the men who looked for gold.

Buck did not like it, but he could do the work and took pride in it the same way Dave and Solleks did. And Buck made sure that his teammates, whether or not they also took pride in it, did their fair share of work. It was a boring life, and one day was very much like another. At a certain time each morning the cooks woke up, built the fires, and cooked breakfast. Then, while some men packed up the camp, others harnessed the dogs, and they were on their way an hour or so before dawn. At night, they made camp again. Some men made fires, others cut firewood, and still others carried water or ice for the cooks. Also, the dogs were fed. To the dogs, this was the most interesting part of the day, but it was also good to loaf around after the fish was eaten for an hour or so with the other dogs. There were dozens of them. There were fierce fighters among them, but after three fights with the fiercest dogs, Buck became an unbeatable fighter. When he bristled and showed his teeth, all the dogs got out of his way.

Perhaps best of all, Buck loved to lie near the fire, hind legs crouched under him, forelegs stretched out in front, head raised, and eyes blinking dreamily at the flames. Sometimes he thought of Judge Miller's big house in the sunny Santa Clara Valley, and of the cement swimming tank, and Ysabel, the Mexican hairless, and Toots, the Japanese pug. But more often he remembered the man in the red sweater, Curly being hurt, the great fight with Spitz, and the good things he had eaten or would like to eat. He was not homesick. The South was far away, and memories of it did not affect him. More important were the instincts he felt. They made things he had never seen seem familiar.

It was a hard trip, with all the mail in the sled, and the work wore all the dogs down. They were weak when they arrived in Dawson, and should have had at least a week or ten days to rest. But after only two days they started down the Yukon River loaded with letters again. The dogs were tired, the drivers grumbling, and to make things worse, it snowed every day. This made the trail soft, so the sled could not slide as easily, which meant even heavier pulling for the dogs. Although it was hard, the drivers were fair through it all, and they did their best for the animals.

Each night the dogs were looked after first. They ate before the drivers ate, and no man set up his sleeping bag until he had looked after the feet of the dogs he drove. Still, their strength went down. Since the beginning of winter they had traveled eighteen hundred miles, dragging sleds the whole distance, and eighteen hundred miles will wear down even the toughest dogs. Buck kept at it, keeping his teammates up to their work and working together, even though he was also very tired. Billee cried and whimpered in his sleep each night. Joe was meaner than ever, and Solleks was unapproachable from any side.

But of all the dogs in the team, it was Dave who suffered most. Something had gone wrong with him. He became more unhappy and angry, and as soon as camp was set up, he would dig his sleeping hole, where his driver fed him. Once out of the harness and lying down, he did not get up again until harness time in the morning. Sometimes, in the harness, when he pulled hard he would cry out in pain. The driver examined him, but could find nothing wrong.

By the time they reached Cassiar Bar, Dave was so weak that he was falling down in the harness. The Scottish driver stopped the dogs and took Dave out of the team. He wanted to rest

Dave and let him run free behind the sled. Sick as he was, Dave did not like being taken out. He grunted and growled while the harness was taken off, and he whimpered sadly when he saw Sol-leks in the position he had held for so long. Dave felt proud of his work, and even though he was sick he could not stand to see another dog do his work.

When the sled started up again, Dave ran in the snow, barking at Sol-leks and trying to push him out of the way. The driver tried to make Dave stay away from the harness but he could not, and this made him very sad. He could see how much Dave wanted to be on the team. Dave refused to run quietly on the trail behind the sled, where the going was easy. He continued to run next to the sled, in the soft snow, where it was more difficult to run, until he was exhausted. Then he lay down and rested while the other sleds passed by.

With the last of his strength, he managed to catch up to the sleds where they had made a rest stop, and he walked past the other sleds until he found his own. Then he stood next to Sol-leks. The driver was away for a few moments, getting a light for his pipe from the man behind them. Then he came back to the sled and started the dogs. They ran out onto the trail easily, turned their heads, and stopped in surprise. The driver was surprised, too. The sled had not moved. He called the other drivers over to see what had happened. Dave had bitten through the harness that connected Sol-leks to the other dogs and to the sled, and was standing right in front of the sled.

He pleaded with his eyes to stay there. The

driver did not know what to do. The other drivers talked about how it could make a dog sad to be taken away from the work that it loved, and they talked about other dogs that had done similar things. They decided that even though Dave was sick and injured, they should let him do the work if he wanted it. So they harnessed him in again, and he pulled as he did before, but more than once he cried out in pain as he worked. Several times he fell down while they ran.

He held out until they set up their camp that night, where the driver made a place for him by the fire. In the morning he was too weak to travel, and the driver had to leave him behind to rest and get better. The last time his teammates saw him, he was lying in the snow and watching them leave on the trail. They could hear him howling sadly until they passed out of sight behind some trees by the river.

CHAPTER 7

New Masters

ᴄᴏ

Thirty days after they left Dawson, Buck and his teammates arrived at Skaguay. They were carrying the Salt Water mail. The dogs were very tired and worn out. Buck normally weighed one hundred and forty pounds, but now he was only one hundred and fifteen. Even though the other dogs were lighter than Buck, they had also lost more weight. Pike, who often pretended to have a hurt leg so he would not have to work, was now limping for real. Sol-leks was also limping, and Dub's shoulder was hurt.

Their legs were all terribly sore. There was no spring or bounce left in them. Their feet felt heavy on the trail. There was nothing wrong with the dogs except that they were dead tired. It was not the kind of tiredness that comes from a small bit of hard work, when it takes only a few hours to recover. This was the kind of tiredness that comes after many long months of hard work. The dogs did not have any strength left. It had all been used—every last bit of it. Every muscle was dead tired. In less than five months they had traveled twenty-five hundred miles, and during the last eighteen hundred miles they had taken only five days of rest. When they arrived at Skaguay, they looked like they were on their last legs. They could barely pull the sled, and on the downhills they just managed to keep out of the way of the sled.

"Mush on, you poor sore feet," the driver encouraged them as they tottered down the main street of Skaguay. "This is the last. Then we will get one long rest, hey? For sure. One very long rest."

The drivers were sure that they would have a long rest. But there were so many men rushing into the Klondike looking for gold, and many of them did not bring their families with them, which meant that there was a lot of mail, along with the official orders. Fresh batches of Hudson Bay dogs were coming in to take the places of those who could not run the trail anymore. The ones who could no longer run were sold.

Three days passed, and Buck and his teammates found out how tired and weak they really were. On the morning of the fourth day, two men from the South came along and bought them, harness and all. The men called each other Hal and Charles. Charles was a middle-aged man, with watery eyes and a mustache that twisted up at the ends. Hal was only nineteen or twenty, and carried a big gun and hunting knife strapped to his belt. Both men were out of place here in the North, and no one could understand why they had come.

Buck heard the men talking, saw the money pass between the man and the government agent, and knew that the Scottish driver and the mail train drivers were passing out of his life just like Perrault and François and the others who had gone before. When they arrived at their new camp, Buck saw a messy place. The tent was falling down, and there were unwashed dishes. He also saw a woman, whom the men called Mercedes. She was Charles's wife and Hal's sister.

Buck watched them nervously as they tried to take down the tent and load the sled. They were trying hard, but they did not know what to do. They rolled the tent into a bundle three times as large as it should have been. They left the dishes unwashed and packed them. Mercedes and the two men talked and argued all the time. When they put a sack of clothes on the front of the sled, she suggested it should go on the back. After they had put it there, and covered it with a few other bundles, she found more things they forgot to pack, and that had to go in the clothes sack, so they unloaded everything and started again.

Three men from a camp nearby came and watched, grinning and winking at each other.

"You have a heavy load already," said one of them. "I shouldn't tell you your business, but I wouldn't take that tent along if I was you."

"Impossible!" Mercedes cried, throwing up her hands. "How in the world could we manage without a tent?"

"You don't need it. It's springtime, and you won't get any more cold weather," the man replied.

She shook her head as Charles and Hal put the last few items on top of the huge load.

"Think it'll ride?" one of the men asked.

"Why shouldn't it?" Charles said angrily.

"Oh, that's all right, that's all right," the man said quickly. "I was just wondering, that's all. It seemed a little top-heavy."

Charles turned his back and pulled the ropes down as well as he could, which was not very well at all.

"And you're sure the dogs can hike all day with that load behind them?" another man asked.

"Certainly," said Hal. "Mush!" he shouted. "Mush on there!"

The dogs sprang forward in the harness, strained hard for a few moments, then relaxed. They could not move the sled.

"Lazy beasts!" Hal shouted. He became angry with the dogs, but Mercedes asked him not to treat them badly.

"The poor dears," she cried. "Now you must promise you won't be harsh with them the rest of the trip, or I won't go a step."

"You don't know anything about dogs," her brother sneered. "They're lazy, I tell you, and you have to be mean to get anything out of them. That's their way. You ask anyone. Ask any one of those men."

"They're weak as water, if you want to know," said one of the men. "Plum tuckered out, that's what's the matter. They need a rest."

"No they don't," Hal said angrily.

"They do if you want them strong enough to do their job," the other man shot back.

"Why don't you leave me alone with them and let me do my job," Hal replied.

"Listen, sir, I'm just trying to give you good advice. Anyone can see these dogs need a rest. But if you don't want to listen to me, you don't have to."

"You said it," Hal answered.

For a moment the other man seemed to grow

angry. Then his face changed and a small smile crossed his lips. "You know," he said, "on second thought I figure you really do know what you're doing." Then he turned his back on Hal and silently walked away.

Mercedes was embarrassed by the scene but happy that it was now over.

"Never mind that man," she said to her brother. "You're driving our dogs, and you do what you think is best."

Hal did everything he could to make the dogs move. They threw themselves forward, dug their feet into the packed snow, got down low to it, and used all their strength. The sled held as though it was an anchor. After two tries, they stood still, panting. Hal was terribly angry with them. He yelled and pushed and shoved them. Then Mercedes stopped him again. She dropped on her knees in front of Buck, with tears in her eyes, and put her arms around his neck.

"You poor, poor dears," she cried. "Why don't you pull hard? Then he won't be so mean to you."

Buck did not like her, but he was feeling too miserable to resist.

One of the onlookers, who had been clenching his teeth because he was so angry, now spoke up.

"It's not that I care what happens to you, but for the dogs' sakes I just want to tell you this. You can help them a lot by breaking that sled out of the ice. It's frozen to the ground. Throw your weight against it, rock it right and left, and break it out."

They tried a third time to move, but this time they followed the man's advice, and Hal managed to break the sled loose from the ice and snow. The overloaded and awkward sled moved forward, with Buck and his teammates struggling under the mean treatment from Hal. A hundred yards ahead, the path turned and went downhill toward the main street. It would have taken an experienced driver to keep the top-heavy sled upright on this turn. Hal did not know how to do it. As they went around the turn, the sled fell over, spilling half its load through the loose ropes. The dogs didn't stop running, and the sled bounced on its side behind them. They were angry because of the bad treatment they had received and the heavy load. Buck was raging mad. He broke into a run, and the team followed him. Hal cried, "Whoa! Whoa!" but they did not stop. He tripped and was pulled off his feet. The dogs dashed up the street, scattering the rest of the load along the way.

Some friendly people caught the dogs and gathered up the belongings. They also gave advice. They told Hal, Charles, and Mercedes to cut their load by half and get twice as many dogs if they ever wanted to reach Dawson as they planned. Hal and his sister and brother-in-law listened unwillingly, pitched their tent, and went through all of their things. They threw away canned food, which made the other men laugh because canned food on the trail is something that people only dream about.

"Those are blankets for a hotel," said one of the men who laughed and helped. "Half as many of these would still be too much. Get rid of them. Throw away that tent and all those dishes. Who's going to wash them anyway? Do you think you're traveling on a fancy train?"

And so it went as they tossed out everything they did not need. Mercedes cried when her clothes bags were dumped on the ground and each piece of clothing was thrown away. She was sad, and after she went through her things, she went through the men's belongings like a tornado.

Even though their load was only half as large now, it was still big. Charles and Hal went out in the evening and bought six dogs, which were not from the North. These, added to the six on the original team, and Teek and Koona, the huskies who were bought at the Rink Rapids on the record trip, brought the team up to fourteen dogs. But the new dogs, even though they had been trained, were not so good. They did not seem to know anything. Buck and his comrades did not like them. He taught the new dogs quickly what they should not do, but he could not teach them what they should do. They were not made for this trail and the hard work that came with it. Most of them were confused and frightened both by the strange environment and by the bad treatment they had received.

With the newcomers hopeless and sad, and the old team worn out by twenty-five hundred miles of continuous running, the outlook was anything but bright. The two men, however, were quite cheerful. And they were proud, too.

They had never seen a sled with fourteen dogs. In the Arctic, there was a good reason why fourteen dogs should not drag one sled, and that was because one sled could not carry enough food for fourteen dogs. But Charles and Hal did not know this. They had figured out everything on paper, planning the amount of food they thought they would need. It had all seemed very simple.

Late next morning Buck led the long team up the street. There was nothing lively about them—no snap or go in him and his fellows. They were starting out dead tired. Four times Buck had covered the distance between Salt Water and Dawson, and the thought that he was going on the same trail once more, when he was so tired already, made him angry. His heart was not in the work. The newcomers were frightened, and the old team did not have confidence in their drivers.

Buck knew the dogs could not depend on

NEW MASTERS

these three people. They did not know how to do anything, and as the days went by it became clear that they could not learn. They were lazy. It took them half the night to set up a messy camp. Then it took them half the morning to pack up and get the sled loaded so badly that for the rest of the day they were busy stopping and rearranging the load. On other days they could not get started at all, so they never got as far each day as the men had planned.

They would run out of dog food soon, and the men made it happen even faster by feeding the dogs too much. The newcomers ate too much, and when the team pulled weakly, Hal decided that it was because they were not eating enough, so he doubled their portions. Then, when Mercedes felt bad for the dogs and could not convince her brother to give them more food, she stole food from the supplies and fed them when the men were not watching. It was not food that

Buck and the huskies needed. They needed rest.

Hal realized one day that his dog food was already half gone, and they were only a short way into their trip. Even worse, no more dog food could be found out there. So he cut down the rations to very little, and tried to increase each day's travel. It was easy to give the dogs less food, but it was impossible to make them travel faster. The men and woman were also getting angry with each other.

One day they finally decided to leave the six new dogs behind to get rested and healed. By this time the three people were rude and angry with each other all the time. Arctic travel was not a fun adventure anymore. All they did was argue. Their muscles ached, their bones ached, and even their hearts ached.

When Charles and Hal argued, it was because each believed he was doing more than his share of work. Sometimes Mercedes agreed with her husband, sometimes with her brother. The result was a family argument that would never end.

Mercedes did not like the trail. She was also used to people helping her. Her husband and her brother, however, did not offer to help. Instead, they complained about her, and she treated them badly in return. She did not care anymore about the dogs, and because she was sore and tired, she insisted on riding on the sled. She was not large, but she did weigh one hundred and twenty pounds, and the extra weight tired the dogs out even more. She rode for days until the dogs fell down and could not pull anymore. Charles and Hal begged her to get off the sled and walk.

Once, they picked her up and took her off the sled. They never did it again. She sat down on the trail and was very upset with them. They went on their way, but Mercedes did not move. After they

had traveled three miles, they unloaded the sled, came back for her, picked her up, and put her back on the sled.

They were treating each other badly, but they treated their animals even worse. Hal was mean to the dogs. When the dog food ran out, he traded the big knife and gun on his belt for some old, frozen meat. It was a poor substitute for food, like trying to eat strips of iron.

Through it all, Buck staggered along at the head of the team as if he were in a nightmare. He pulled when he could, and when he could not, he fell down and stayed down while the people pushed and shoved him until he could get up again. All the stiffness and shine had gone out of his beautiful furry coat. The hair hung down and was matted together in clumps. His muscles were gone, and he was so skinny that every rib and bone of his body was outlined through his skin. It was heartbreaking, but Buck's heart was un-breakable.

Buck's team was in just as bad shape as Buck was. They looked like walking skeletons. There were seven altogether, including Buck. When they stopped, they would drop in the harness as if they were dead.

There came a day when Billee fell, could not continue, and had to be left behind. On the next day, Koona also had to be left behind, and only five of them remained: Joe, too tired to be mean; Pike, limping and sore; Sol-leks, the one-eyed, still wanting to work, and sad that he did not have more strength; Teek, who had not traveled far that winter and who was now even more tired than the others; and Buck, still at the head of the team, but too tired to do anything and able to stay on the trail only by the feel of his feet.

CHAPTER 8

John Thornton

✧

Although it was beautiful spring weather, the dogs and humans did not notice it. Each day the sun rose earlier and set later. It was dawn by three in the morning, and stayed light until nine at night.

From every hill came the trickle of running water. The ice was beginning to melt everywhere. Airholes formed in the ice, cracks opened and spread apart, while thin sections of ice fell through into the river underneath.

With the dogs falling, Mercedes crying, Hal

yelling angrily, and Charles's eyes watering, they staggered into John Thornton's camp at the mouth of White River. When they stopped, the dogs dropped to the ground. Mercedes dried her eyes and looked at John Thornton. Charles sat on a log to rest. He sat very slowly and carefully because his body was so stiff. Hal did the talking. John Thornton was whittling an ax handle. He whittled and listened, gave short replies and, when asked, even shorter pieces of advice. He knew what these people were like right away, and when he gave his advice he was sure they would not follow it.

"They told us that the ice was breaking on the trail, the bottom dropping out, and the best thing for us to do was to wait," Hal said, after Thornton warned them not to risk going over the ice. "They told us we couldn't make it to White River, and here we are."

"And they told you the truth," John

Thornton answered, "The bottom's going to drop out at any moment. Only fools, with the blind luck of fools, could have made it this far. I wouldn't risk my life on that ice for all the gold in Alaska."

"That's because you're not a fool, I suppose," said Hal. "All the same, we'll go on to Dawson. Get up there, Buck! Hey, get up there! Mush on!"

Thornton went on whittling. He knew it was a waste of time to try to stop a fool, and two or three less fools in the world would not be such a bad thing.

But the team did not get up at Hal's command. He pushed and kicked the dogs, and used his whip. John Thornton pressed his lips together tightly. Sol-leks was the first to crawl to his feet. Teek followed. Joe came next, yelping with pain. Pike fell over twice before he was able to stand. Buck made no effort. He lay quietly where he had fallen. No matter what Hal did, Buck did not move. Neither did he whine or struggle. Several times, Thornton started to speak, but changed his mind. As Hal continued to treat Buck badly, Thornton stood and walked back and forth.

This was the first time Buck had failed, and this made Hal very angry. Buck still refused to move. Like his teammates, he was barely able to get up. He had made up his mind not to get up. He had a feeling that something bad was going to happen. He felt it when they stopped at John Thornton's camp. All day, the thin ice under his feet had seemed like it was about to break. He was experienced and smart enough to recognize the feeling. He refused to move. He had suffered so much, and he was so tired, that nothing hurt him now, even Hal's blows.

Suddenly, without warning, John Thornton jumped at Hal and knocked him backward. Mercedes screamed. Charles looked on sadly, wiped his eyes, but did not get up because of his stiffness. John Thornton stood over Buck and struggled to control himself, too angry to speak.

"If you hurt that dog again, I'll hit you again," he finally said.

"It's my dog," Hal replied, wiping his mouth as he came back. "Get out of my way, or I'll fix you. I'm going to Dawson."

"Not with that dog," Thornton said.

"Be careful, Hal," Mercedes cried out in fear. "We don't want any trouble."

"You keep out of this," Hal answered her.

All this while Thornton stood between Hal and Buck and made no move to get out of the way. Hal lifted his whip. Thornton hit Hal's knuckles with the ax handle, knocking the whip to the ground. He rapped Hal's knuckles again as he tried to pick it up. Thornton stooped, picked it up, and threw it away. Then he took out his knife and cut Buck loose from the harness.

Hal was too tired to fight, and Buck was

too tired to keep on the team, anyway.

"All right," Hal finally said to Thornton. "You win. Keep that worthless dog. We don't need him anyway."

A few minutes later they pulled out from the camp and along the ice that covered the river. Buck heard them go and raised his head to watch. The dogs were limping and staggering. Mercedes was riding the sled. Hal guided, and Charles stumbled along behind them.

Thornton knelt beside Buck and with rough, kind hands searched for any injuries. He and Buck watched the sled on the ice. Suddenly, they saw its back end drop down. They heard Mercedes scream, saw Charles turn and make a step to run back, and then a whole section of ice gave way as the dogs and humans disappeared. The ice had broken. The bottom had dropped out of the trail.

They saw the team struggle out without the sled or any of their belongings. They dragged themselves and the dogs to the far bank. Without calling to Thornton for help, the team started back in the direction they had come from, toward the next camp, where they would dry off and warm up before heading back home.

John Thornton and Buck looked at each other.

"You poor devil," said John Thornton, and Buck licked his hand.

The previous December, John Thornton's feet had gotten wet and they had frozen in the cold. His partners had made him comfortable and then left him to get well while they traveled up the river to get a raft headed for Dawson. He was still limping a little when he rescued Buck, but as the weather became warmer, he stopped limping.

Like John Thornton, Buck used these days to heal. Lying by the riverbank through the long spring afternoons, watching the running water, and listening to the songs of birds and the hum of nature, he slowly won back his strength.

A rest feels good after traveling three thousand miles, and Buck felt lazy as his wounds healed, his muscles swelled out, and the flesh came back to cover his bones. They were all feeling lazy—Buck, John Thornton, Skeet, and Vig—waiting for the raft to come and carry them down to Dawson. Skeet was a smaller dog, and she made friends quickly with Buck, who was too tired to turn her away. She was like a doctor to him; in much the same way that a mother cat washes her kittens, Skeet would wash and clean Buck's wounds. Each morning after he had finished his breakfast, she took care of him, until he began to look forward to these treatments. As for Vig, he was a huge black dog. Vig was just as friendly as Skeet, but he did not show it as much.

To Buck's surprise, these dogs never treated him badly or competed with him. They seemed to be just as kind and generous as John Thornton.

Buck started to feel love for the first time. He had never experienced it at Judge Miller's house down in the sunny Santa Clara Valley. With the Judge's sons, when they hunted together, he had felt like a partner. With the Judge's grandsons, he had felt like a guardian. And with the Judge, he had felt like a friend. But Buck felt love for John Thornton.

This man had saved his life—Buck knew he would not have survived the trail with Hal, Charles, and Mercedes. John Thornton was also the best master. Other men looked after their dogs because it made sense. Thornton looked after his as if they were his own children, because he could not help it.

And he did more. He always spoke kindly with them. He had a way of taking Buck's head roughly between his hands, resting his own head on Buck's, and shaking him back and forth. While he did this, he would call Buck bad names, just for fun. Buck knew nothing better than that rough embrace and the sound of Thornton's words. At each shake it seemed like Buck's heart would be shaken out of his body because he felt so much happiness. And when Thornton let go, Buck sprang to his feet, his mouth laughing and his eyes bright, and stood still. John Thornton would stare at him and say, "Boy, you can all but speak!"

Buck showed his love in a way that was almost like being angry. He would often take Thornton's hand in his mouth and pretend to bite. Buck understood that Thornton called him bad names just for fun, and Thornton understood these pretend bites were like a hug.

Buck went wild with happiness when Thornton touched him or spoke to him, but Buck did not chase after this. Skeet was different, and would shove her nose under Thornton's hand and nudge and nudge until he petted her.

Vig would stalk up and rest his large head on Thornton's knee. Buck was happy to adore Thornton at a distance. He would lie and wait at Thornton's feet, eager and alert, looking up into his face and studying it—interested in every expression, every movement or change. Or he would lie farther away, watching the movements of Thornton's body. The man and dog were so close that when Buck would stare at him, Thornton would feel it, turn his head, and stare back without speaking.

For a long time after his rescue, Buck did not even like Thornton to get out of his sight. And so Buck followed him everywhere. All of the previous masters had left him, and he was afraid that Thornton would leave, just as Perrault and François and the Scottish driver had left. Even at night in his dreams he was afraid. When this happened, he would shake off sleep and creep through the cold night to the flap of the tent. There he would stand and listen to the sound of his master's breathing.

Even though he felt great love toward John Thornton, Buck also felt wild and sneaky from his life on the trail. Because of his great love, he could not steal from this man. But from any other man, in any other camp, he would not wait a moment to steal, and his great cunning allowed him to do it without ever getting caught.

His face and body were scarred from all of his fights with other dogs, and he still fought as fiercely as ever. Skeet and Vig were too friendly to fight with him, and besides, they belonged to John Thornton. But Buck tried to fight with any other dog he met.

He looked and felt older than he really was. He was becoming more and more like a wild dog. Sometimes, sitting by the fire next to John Thornton, Buck would feel the urge to run into the dark forest. He did not know where he was going, or why he had to run, but he knew he had to do it. Then, he would remember his love for John Thornton and return to the fire again.

Thornton was the only thing that kept Buck from running away. All other people meant nothing to him. Travelers might pet him, but he did not care, and from an overly friendly man he would get up and walk away. When Thornton's partners, Hans and Pete, finally arrived on their raft, Buck refused to notice them until he learned they were close to Thornton. After that, he behaved like he was doing them a favor by letting them be nice to him. By the time their raft arrived at Dawson, they understood Buck and his ways, and they did not try to be as friendly with him as they were with Skeet and Vig.

For Thornton, however, his love seemed to grow and grow. Thornton was the only man who could put a pack on Buck's back when they traveled in the summer. Nothing was too great for Buck to do if Thornton asked him to do it. One day, the men and dogs were sitting near the edge of a cliff that went straight down into a rocky canyon three hundred feet below. John Thornton was sitting closest to the edge, Buck at his shoulder. Thornton had an idea. He asked Hans and Pete just how devoted they thought Buck was to him.

"I've never seen a dog so loyal," Hans said as Pete nodded his head in agreement.

"Let me show you just how loyal he really is," Thornton said. "Watch this."

Thornton turned to Buck, who had kept his eyes on his master the whole time.

"Jump, Buck!" he commanded, pointing out and over the cliff.

The next instant, he was pulling Buck back from the edge, with Hans and Pete helping him.

"It's amazing," Pete said, after it was over and they were all safe.

Thornton shook his head. "No. It is good that he would listen to me, but it is terrible, too. Sometimes it makes me afraid."

"I would not want to be the man who lays hands on you while he's around," Pete said, nodding his head toward Buck. "He's as loyal and fierce a friend anyone could have."

"By jingo!" Hans chimed in. "I agree with Pete. That dog is worth an army. I pity the man who has to find that out the hard way."

It was at Circle City, before the end of the year, that Pete's worries came true. "Black" Burton was a bad-tempered and mean man, and he had been picking a fight with a newcomer at the hotel when Thornton stepped in to break them up. Buck was lying in the corner, as he always did, head on his paws, watching every move his master made. Burton struck out, without warning, and knocked Thornton over.

The people who were watching heard a sound

that was not a bark or a yelp, but something that was closer to a roar, and they saw Buck rise in the air as he jumped on Burton. Burton was hurled back with Buck on top of him. The crowd had to pull Buck away, and while they checked Burton's injuries, Buck prowled up and down, growling furiously, trying to rush in and being forced back by dozens of men.

Finally, Burton was able to stagger back onto his feet. "I've never seen a dog like that," he gasped, "and I pray I will never see another one like him again." From that day on, Buck's name spread through every camp in Alaska.

Later on, in the fall of that year, he saved John Thornton's life in a very different way. The three partners were trying to move a small boat past the rapids on Forty Mile Creek. Hans and Pete were on the land, holding a rope that was attached to the boat. Thornton was in the boat, moving it carefully across the river and shouting

directions to the men on shore. Buck was on the land worried, watching the boat.

At a bad spot, the boat and the rope became tangled, and the boat flipped over. Thornton was swept downstream into the worst part of the rapids.

Buck jumped in at that very moment, and, in the mad swirl of water, managed to catch Thornton. When he felt him grasp his tail, Buck headed for the shore, swimming with all his strength. But it was slow going, and the rapids were too strong. Thornton knew it would be impossible to reach the shore. He tried to hold on to the rocks, missed several times, and then caught hold of one. He let go of Buck and above the roar of the water shouted, "Go, Buck! Go!"

Buck was pulled farther downstream and could not swim back to his master. When he heard Thornton command him again, he turned and headed toward the land. He swam powerfully,

and was pulled ashore by Hans and Pete.
They knew Thornton could not hold on to
the rock for long, and they ran upstream quickly.
They tied a rope to Buck, and he jumped in. He
swam toward Thornton but aimed wrong and
missed him. Hans pulled Buck back to shore. He
lay there, exhausted from swimming in the
rapids, but as soon as he heard Thornton's
voice, Buck sprang to his feet and ran back up
the shoreline.

He jumped in again with the rope attached to
him, and this time he knew how to avoid making
the same mistake. He swam until the current
pulled him toward Thornton, who put his arms
around Buck's shaggy neck. Then Hans and Pete
pulled on the rope. Buck and Thornton were
pulled underwater, where they crashed into the
rocks until they reached the shore.

Thornton woke up first, being shaken by Hans
and Pete, and the first thing he did was look for

Buck. Vig and Skeet were standing over Buck, who was lying on the ground and breathing heavily. Even though he was also hurt badly, Thornton went carefully over Buck's body to check for injuries, and he found that Buck had three broken ribs.

"That settles it," he said. "We camp right here." And camp they did, until Buck's ribs healed and he was able to travel again.

CHAPTER 9

The Bet

⌒

That winter in Dawson, Buck did another amazing thing that made him even more famous. It all started during a conversation in the Eldorado Hotel, where some men were telling each other about their favorite dogs. Buck was the most famous, but these men said that he was not so great. Thornton argued with them. One man said that his dog could pull a sled with five hundred pounds on it. Another man said six hundred for his dog, and a third said seven hundred.

"That's nothing," said John Thornton. "Buck

can pull a sled with a thousand pounds on it."

"And break it out of the ice? And walk off with it for a hundred yards?" asked Matthewson, who had claimed seven hundred pounds for his dog.

"And break it out and walk off with it for a hundred yards," John Thornton said, coolly.

"Well," Matthewson said, slowly and deliberately, so everyone could hear, "I've got a thousand dollars that says he can't. And there it is." He slammed a sack of gold dust the size of a sausage on the bar.

Nobody spoke. Thornton could feel himself blush. He had spoken too soon. He did not know if Buck could pull that much. A thousand pounds! The size of it made him feel sick. He was certain that Buck had great strength, and he had thought many times that Buck might be able to pull such a load. But now he had to do it. The whole town was waiting and watching. Even worse, Thornton did not have a thousand dollars. Neither did Hans, nor Pete.

"I've got a sled standing outside now, with twenty fifty-pound sacks of flour on it," Matthewson went on, sounding mean. "That's a thousand pounds. So we can go right now."

Thornton did not reply. He did not know what to say. He looked from face to face, and saw an old friend, Jim O'Brien.

"Can you lend me a thousand?" Thornton asked, almost in a whisper.

"Sure," answered O'Brien, thumping down a sack right next to Matthewson's. "I'm putting my faith in you, John, that the beast can do the trick."

"Don't worry, that dog can do miracles," Thornton said. "He even saved my life, once."

"And he'd do it again," Pete said. Thinking back to the time when Buck almost jumped over the cliff on Thornton's command, he added, "I've never seen a dog so devoted to his master. If Buck can't do it, it can't be done."

O'Brien nodded his head in agreement. "I've heard about this one and what he can do," he said, pointing to Buck. "I know it's a risk, but it's a risk I'm willing to take. Matthewson is a big talker, but Buck's the one who can get things done."

Everyone left the Eldorado and stood on the street outside. Several hundred men, wearing furs and mittens, stood around Matthewson's sled. It was loaded with a thousand pounds of flour and had been sitting there for several hours. In the cold, the sled had frozen to the hard-packed snow. Most men were betting that Buck could not budge the sled.

Even John Thornton felt terrible that he had rushed into the bet once he looked at the sled, with its regular team of ten dogs lying in the snow in front of it. Buck's task seemed next to impossible. Matthewson, however, was happy.

"Three to one!" he yelled. "I'll bet you another thousand at that figure, Thornton. What do you say?"

Thornton looked worried, but his fighting spirit was aroused. He called Hans and Pete to him. Together, the three men had only two hundred dollars. It was everything they had, and they bet it all.

The team of ten dogs was unhitched, and Buck, with his own harness, was connected to the sled. He had felt the excitement around him, and he knew that in some way he had to do a great thing for John Thornton. The crowd talked about how great Buck looked. He was in perfect shape, one hundred and fifty pounds of pure strength, and his furry coat shone like silk. Men felt his muscles and said they were as hard as iron, and the odds went down to two to one.

"By God, sir!" exclaimed one member of the crowd to Thornton, "I'll offer you eight hundred for him, sir, before the test of strength. Eight hundred for him right now."

Thornton shook his head and stepped to Buck's side.

"You must stay away from him as he pulls," Matthewson said. "Give him plenty of room."

The crowd fell silent. Everybody agreed that Buck was a magnificent animal, but they thought one thousand pounds was just too much for one dog to pull, and no one else would bet that he could do it.

Thornton knelt next to Buck. He took his head in his two hands and rested his cheek on Buck's. He did not playfully shake his head or call him names, as Buck would have liked him to do. Instead, he whispered in Buck's ear.

"As you love me, Buck. As you love me," was what he whispered. Buck whined with eagerness that he could barely hold inside.

The crowd was watching curiously. It seemed

like something magical was happening. As Thornton stood, Buck grabbed his hand between his jaws, pressing in with his teeth and releasing slowly. It was his answer, showing how much he loved the man. Thornton stepped back. "Now, Buck," he said.

Buck tightened the harness and then let it go loose by a few inches. It was the way he had learned to do it.

"Gee!" Thornton yelled. It was one of the special calls drivers used with their dogs.

Buck swung to the right, pulling the harness tight with a sudden jerk. The sled shook, and there was the sound of ice crackling.

"Haw!" Thornton commanded.

Buck jumped again, this time to the left. The crackling turned into a snapping sound, and the sled moved several inches to the side. The sled was broken out of the ice. Men were holding their breaths without knowing it.

"Now, *mush!*"

Thornton's command cracked out like a gun-shot. Buck threw himself forward, tightening the harness straps. His whole body shook from the effort, his muscles tightening and moving under the silky fur. His great chest was close to the ground, his head forward and down, while his feet were moving fast, the claws scraping the hard-packed snow. The sled trembled and started a small bit forward. One of his feet slipped and one man groaned. Then the sled lurched ahead in a series of jerks, and never came to a stop again. Half an inch, an inch, two inches. The jerks ended as the sled gained speed, until it was moving steadily.

Men gasped and began to breathe again. Thornton was running behind, cheering Buck on. The distance for the bet had been marked with a pile of firewood, and a cheer began to grow, and it turned into a roar as Buck passed the

firewood and stopped at Thornton's command.
Every man was throwing his hat and mittens in
the air, even Matthewson. Men were shaking
hands with each other and laughing.

But Thornton was on his knees beside Buck.
Their heads were against each other, and he was
shaking him back and forth. The men who hurried up to them heard him calling Buck bad
names in a soft, loving voice.

"By God, sir! Sir!" sputtered the man who had offered to buy Buck. "I'll give you a thousand for him, sir. A thousand, sir. Make it twelve hundred, sir."

Thornton stood silently. His eyes were wet, and tears were streaming down his face.

"Fourteen hundred, then," the man cried.

"No, sir," Thornton said when he finally felt able to speak. "Not for all the gold in Alaska."

Buck seized Thornton's hand again in his teeth. Thornton shook Buck's head back and forth. The crowd moved back from them, and no one interrupted them again.

By winning the bet, Buck earned sixteen hundred dollars in five minutes for John Thornton. The money made it possible for Thornton to pay off his debts and to travel with his partners into the East after a famous lost mine. Many men had searched for it, and there were many stories told about it. No one knew who had found it first.

There had been talk of an old cabin that was near the mine. There were gold nuggets that people said were from there, and they were different from gold found anywhere else in the North.

John Thornton, Pete, and Hans took Buck and half a dozen other dogs with them and headed east on an unknown trail to find the lost mine. They traveled seventy miles up the Yukon River, swung to the left into the Stewart River, passed the Mayo and McQuestion Rivers, and kept going until the Stewart was nothing but a small stream in the tall mountains.

John Thornton did not need much to survive, and he was not afraid of the wild. With a handful of salt and a rifle, he could plunge into the wilderness and live as long as he wanted. He was in no hurry and hunted like the natives while he traveled. If he could not catch his dinner, then like the natives he would keep on traveling, certain that sooner or later he would catch something.

So, on this great journey into the East, the men and dogs ate meat regularly. The sled was loaded with ammunition and tools, and they took their time traveling.

Buck loved all this hunting, fishing, and wandering through strange places. For weeks at a time they would travel, day after day. For weeks on end they would camp, here and there, the dogs being lazy and the men burning holes through the ice and gravel, and panning for gold by the heat of the fire. Sometimes they went hungry; sometimes they ate until they were full. Summer arrived, and the dogs and men carried packs on their backs, rode rafts across mountain lakes, and traveled along rivers in small boats they made from trees in the forest.

Months came and went, and their path twisted back and forth through the land where no men lived. They wandered on the old trails through the winter, and in the spring they finally found something. It was not the lost mine or the lost cabin but a shallow river in a deep valley. The rocks in this river were full of gold. The team stopped searching and stayed there. Each day they found thousands of dollars' worth of gold dust and nuggets in the river. They put the gold in sacks, fifty pounds to each bag, and piled them like firewood outside of the small cabin they had made.

There was nothing for the dogs to do but haul in the game that Thornton caught. So Buck spent many hours dreaming by the fire. Buck dreamed that he could hear something calling to him from the forest. He felt happy, and he wanted to do something important, but he did not know what it was. Sometimes he chased the call into the forest, looking for it as if it were an animal. He would push his nose into the cool moss or into the black soil where long grasses grew. Or he would crouch for hours, hiding behind the trunks of fallen trees, watching and listening to everything that moved or made a sound near him. He did not know why he was doing these things. He only knew that he had to do them, and he did not ask himself why.

Sometimes he would be lying in camp, sleeping in the heat of the day, when suddenly he would lift his head as if he had heard something. Then he would spring to his feet and dash away. On and on for hours, through the forest and across open spaces he would run. He would lie in the bushes for days at a time, where he could watch the birds. He loved to run at midnight in the summertime. Buck always kept looking for the mysterious thing that called for him to come.

CHAPTER 10

The Call of the Wild

ᕲᔍ

One night Buck woke up suddenly and sniffed the air, his hair bristling. From the forest came a call that was different than before. It was a long, drawn-out howl. He sprang through the camp, where everyone was still asleep, and ran through the woods. As he moved closer to the cry, he went slowly and carefully until he came to an open place among the trees. There Buck saw a long, lean timber wolf, sitting on its hind legs, with its nose pointed to the sky.

Buck made no noise, but the wolf stopped

howling and looked around. Buck walked into the open, half crouching, his body poised and ready to jump, tail straight and stiff. Buck wanted to show that he could be friendly, but the wolf ran away. Buck followed and easily caught up to him. The wolf whirled around, ready to fight.

Buck did not attack. Instead, he circled around the wolf and tried to show that he was friendly. The wolf was suspicious and afraid. Buck was at least three times larger than the wolf, and the wolf's head barely reached Buck's shoulder. When he saw a chance, the wolf ran away and Buck chased him again. Buck always caught up to him, and he ran again, until he was tired.

In the end Buck got what he wanted. The wolf, finding that he was not in danger, finally sniffed noses with him. They became friendly and played with each other in a nervous, shy way. After some time, the wolf started off at an easy run. He wanted Buck to come along, and they ran side by side through the night, into the mountains.

They ran for days, and Buck was happy. He knew he was finally answering the call, running next to his friend, who was like a brother to him. They stopped by a stream to drink, and then Buck remembered John Thornton. He sat down. The wolf started on, and then returned to him, sniffing noses and trying to encourage Buck to keep going. But Buck turned around and started slowly back. For an hour the wolf ran by his side, whining softly. Then he sat down, pointed his nose upward, and howled. It was a sad howl, and as Buck kept going, he heard it grow fainter until it was lost in the distance.

John Thornton was eating dinner when Buck ran into camp and jumped on him, licking his face, biting his hand in their friendly way, while Thornton shook Buck back and forth and called him names.

For two days and nights Buck never left camp, never let Thornton out of his sight. He followed him everywhere, watched him while he ate, saw him into his blankets at night and out of them in the morning. But after two days Buck began to feel the strange call in the forest stronger than ever. Buck's restlessness came back, and he could not stop thinking about the wolf and their run through the forest. Once again he took to wandering in the woods, but the wolf was not there.

He began to go out at night, staying away from camp for days at a time. Once he crossed over the mountain and wandered for a week, looking for the wolf, hunting and eating as he traveled. He never seemed to get tired. He fished for salmon in a stream, and he even won a fight against a large black bear. It was a hard battle, and it made Buck feel like a fighter again. Two days later, he hunted wolverines and caught two of them.

He felt like the best hunter in the world, the

strongest animal. He was proud, and it showed in the way he moved. Except for the brown color on his nose and above his eyes, and the white hair across his chest, he looked like a gigantic wolf, larger than the largest wolf in the world. Buck's father was a St. Bernard, so Buck inherited his size and weight from him, while he had inherited his shape from his mother, who was a shepherd. His nose was long like a wolf's, but it was larger than the nose on any wolf. His head was shaped like a wolf's head, but it was three times larger.

He was as cunning as a wolf, and he was as smart as a shepherd and a St. Bernard. All this, plus the experience gained in the North, made him as strong as any animal that was in the wild. He could respond to sights and sounds as fast as lightning. As quick as a husky dog could leap, he could leap twice as fast. He could see a movement, or hear a sound, and respond in less time than another dog needed just to see or hear something. His muscles were powerful, and they snapped like steel springs.

"There has never been such a dog," said John Thornton one day, as he and his partners watched Buck marching out of camp.

"After he was made, the mold was broke," said Pete.

"By jingo! I think so myself," Hans agreed.

They saw him marching out of camp, but they did not see what changed as soon as he was hidden in the forest. He stopped marching. He became a thing of the wild, creeping softly. He knew how to hide, to crawl on his belly like a snake, and, like a snake, to leap and to strike. He could catch birds in their nests, rabbits as they slept, or squirrels in the air as they jumped. Fish were not fast enough to escape him. Sometimes he enjoyed sneaking up on squirrels, and when he almost had them, he would let them go and watch them run away in fear to the treetops.

As the fall came on, more and more moose appeared, moving slowly down the valley. Buck had already hunted a small one, but he wanted a larger and more difficult animal to catch, and he found it one day near the creek. Twenty moose were traveling there, and their leader was a great bull moose with a mean temper. He stood over six feet tall, and his great antlers were seven feet from tip to tip. His small eyes burned and he roared with fury when he saw Buck.

Buck hunted and chased the moose for days, and while he did this, he felt a change happening in the land. Other kinds of life were coming in. He could feel it in the air. He did not see or hear anything special, but he knew that the land was somehow different, that strange things were wandering there. He decided to give up hunting the moose and investigate. He started back to the camp and to John Thornton. He broke into a run, and went on hour after hour, never losing his way, heading straight home.

While Buck ran he became more and more aware of something new. There was something alive in it, different from what was there in the summer. The birds talked about it, the squirrels chatted about it, and he could smell it in the wind. Several times he stopped and sniffed the air in the morning, as if reading a message, and it made him run even faster. He felt that something bad was happening, or that it had already happened, and as he dropped down into the valley toward camp, he moved carefully.

Three miles away, Buck found a new trail that made his neck hair bristle. It led straight toward camp and John Thornton. Buck hurried on, swiftly and silently, every nerve alert to what he sensed. All the animals in the forest were quietly hiding.

He followed a new scent into a bush. From the camp came the faint sound of many voices, rising and falling in a singsong chant. Creeping closer, Buck looked to where the cabin should have been and saw something that made the hair on his neck and shoulders stand up.

A tribe of natives known as the Yeehats were dancing around the cabin, which had been burned down. Thornton and his partners had set up camp in the natives' territory without knowing that they would be seen as invaders. The Yeehats had attacked and won the fight easily. They were celebrating their victory when they heard a roar and saw an animal rush at them that they had never seen before. It was Buck, hurling himself at them like a hurricane. He chased and hunted them, and it was impossible to fight him off. He was moving too fast, and he was terribly angry. The Yeehats panicked and ran into the woods, calling Buck an "evil spirit." And Buck felt evil as he chased after them. After some time, Buck returned to the camp, which had been destroyed. The men and dogs were gone. Buck could smell the place where Thornton had fought and lost.

All day Buck roamed around the camp, but he did not know what he should do. He only knew that John Thornton was gone. It left an empty space in him that was like hunger, but it ached and ached, and he knew that food could not fill it up.

Sometimes, he felt proud that he had been able to chase away the men who had invaded the camp. He had hunted men, and he realized that they had been easier than the other animals he had hunted. Men were only dangerous when they held weapons. From then on, he would never be afraid of men again, unless they held ropes, arrows, or guns.

At night, a full moon rose high over the trees.

While Buck lay sadly near the water, he sensed something else moving in the forest. He stood up, listening and sniffing the air. Far away there came a faint yelp, followed by several more yelps. They grew closer and louder. It was another call, and this time Buck was ready to follow it. John Thornton was gone. Buck had no more connections to the world of men.

A pack of wolves entered the clearing, and in the center of it, waiting for them, stood Buck. They were amazed. He was so large that they stood still for a moment and stared at him. Then the bravest one of them leaped straight at Buck. Like a flash, Buck fought back. More and more of them tried to attack him, and he fought all of them off.

He did so well that after half an hour, the wolves retreated. They were tired and hurt. Some were lying down, others stood watching Buck, and others were drinking from the water. One wolf, long and lean and gray, approached cautiously, in a friendly way, and Buck recognized him as the one he had met before. He was whining softly, and as Buck whined, they touched noses. Then an old wolf, thin and battle-scarred, came forward. Buck also sniffed noses with him. Then the old wolf sat down, pointed his nose at the moon, and let out a long wolf howl. The others sat down and howled. And now the call came to Buck, too. He sat down and howled with them. After that, the pack crowded around him, sniffing in a half-friendly, half-savage way. The leaders carried the youngest ones and ran away into the woods. The wolves followed, yelping together. And Buck ran with them, side by side with his wild friend, yelping as he ran.

And here may well end the story of Buck. The dog who had once loved nothing more than to lie in the sun in Judge Miller's big house in the lush Santa Clara Valley was now long gone.

But in the years afterward, the Yeehats noticed a change in the wolves. Some now had splashes of brown on their head and nose, or had a white patch along their chest. The Yeehats also tell stories of a Ghost Dog that runs at the head of the pack. They are afraid of this Ghost Dog because it is smarter than any animal or man and can steal from their camps, rob their traps, and escape their best hunters.

Each fall, as the Yeehats move through their territory, there is a valley that they never enter. And they tell sad stories of how an evil spirit came one year and chose to live in that valley.

In the summers there is one animal that travels out of that valley. It is a great wolf that is larger than any other. He crosses through the forest and comes down into an open space among the trees. Here yellow dust and rocks lie on the ground around old broken sacks, with long grass growing around them and hiding them. Here the great wolf thinks and mourns for a while, howling once, long and sad. Then he leaves.

But he is not always alone. When the long winter nights come and the wolves follow their prey into the valleys, he can sometimes be seen running at the head of the pack through the moonlight, leaping above the other wolves, his great throat howling as he sings the song of the pack.

What Do *You* Think?
Questions for Discussion

∽

Have you ever been around a toddler who keeps asking the question "Why?" Does your teacher call on you in class with questions from your homework? Do your parents ask you questions at the dinner table about your day ? We are always surrounded by questions that need a specific response. But is it possible to have a question with no right answer?

The following questions are about the book you just read. But this is not a quiz! They are designed to help you look at the people, places, and events in the story from different angles.

These questions do not have specific answers. Instead, they might make you think of the story in a completely new way.

Think carefully about each question and enjoy discovering more about this classic story.

1. Buck is captured because he follows a man he knows and trusts. How does this betrayal of his trust alter Buck's character? Have you ever been betrayed by someone you trusted?

2. Buck's reaction the first time he sees snow causes everyone to laugh at him. Have you ever had a similar reaction to something new? How did everyone else respond?

3. The author writes of Buck, "When, on cold nights, he pointed his nose at a star and howled long, like a wolf, it felt like one of his ancestors was howling through the centuries, and through him." What do you think this means? Have you ever felt a similar connection to your ancestors?

4. Part of the book deals with how Buck tries to gain control of the other dogs and remove Spitz as leader of the pack. If you were in Buck's pack, would you want to lead the pack or be a part of the group of dogs?

5. The dogs in the story have very different personalities. For instance, Billee is good-natured and Joe is brooding and sour. How are the dogs' personalities like those of your friends and other people you know?

6. Throughout the book, Buck learns a series of hard lessons. How does each lesson help him to better survive in the real world? Have you ever learned a hard lesson that helped you in a later situation?

7. When Hal begins to beat the dogs, Mercedes cries and says to Buck, "Why don't you pull hard? Then he won't be so mean to you." How does Mercedes's treatment of the dogs differ from the way Hal treats them? Are Mercedes and Hal

intentionally cruel to the dogs or do they just not understand their limitations?

8. Why does Buck express unconditional love and loyalty to John Thornton? Have you ever felt this way about someone? Why and to whom?

9. By the end of the book, Buck has undergone extreme changes. How is he different from the beginning of the book? Are these changes for the better or for the worse?

10. The tale of the Ghost Dog describes an animal that is smarter than either animal or man. Do you believe in legends? Do you believe that Buck is the Ghost Dog? Why or why not?

Afterword

by Arthur Pober, EdD

⟶

First impressions are important.

Whether we are meeting new people, going to new places, or picking up a book unknown to us, first impressions count for a lot. They can lead to warm, lasting memories or can make us shy away from any future encounters.

Can you recall your own first impressions and earliest memories of reading the classics?

Do you remember wading through pages and pages of text to prepare for an exam? Or were you the child who hid under the blanket to read with a flashlight, joining forces with Robin Hood to save Maid Marian? Do you remember only how long it took you to read a lengthy novel such as *Little Women*? Or did you become best friends with the March sisters?

Even for a gifted young reader, getting through long chapters with dense language can easily become overwhelming and can obscure the richness of the story and its characters. Reading an abridged, newly crafted version of a classic novel can be the gentle introduction a child needs to explore the characters and story line without the frustration of difficult vocabulary and complex themes.

Reading an abridged version of a classic novel gives the young reader a sense of independence and the satisfaction of finishing a "grown-up" book. And when a child is engaged with and inspired by a classic story, the tone is set for further exploration of the story's themes, characters, history, and details. As a child's reading skills advance, the desire to tackle the original, unabridged version of the story will naturally emerge.

If made accessible to young readers, these stories can become invaluable tools for understanding themselves in the context of their families and social environments. This is why the Classic Starts series includes questions that stimulate discussion regarding the impact and social relevance of the characters and stories today. These questions can foster lively conversations between children and their parents or teachers. When we look at the issues, values, and standards of past times in terms of how we live now, we can appreciate literature's classic tales in a very personal and engaging way.

Share your love of reading the classics with a young child, and introduce an imaginary world real enough to last a lifetime.

Dr. Arthur Pober, EdD

Dr. Arthur Pober has spent more than twenty years in the fields of early-childhood and gifted education. He is the former principal of one of the world's oldest laboratory schools for gifted youngsters, Hunter College Elementary School, and former director of Magnet Schools for the Gifted and Talented for more than 25,000 youngsters in New York City.

Dr. Pober is a recognized authority in the areas of media and child protection and is currently the U.S. representative to the European Institute for the Media and European Advertising Standards Alliance.

Explore these wonderful stories in our Classic Starts™ library.

20,000 Leagues Under the Sea

The Adventures of Huckleberry Finn

The Adventures of Robin Hood

The Adventures of Sherlock Holmes

The Adventures of Tom Sawyer

Anne of Green Gables

Arabian Nights

Around the World in 80 Days

Black Beauty

The Call of the Wild

Dracula

Frankenstein

Gulliver's Travels

Heidi

The Hunchback of Notre-Dame

The Jungle Book

The Last of the Mohicans

Little Lord Fauntleroy

A Little Princess

Little Women

The Man in the Iron Mask

Oliver Twist

The Phantom of the Opera

Pinocchio

Pollyanna

The Prince and the Pauper

Rebecca of Sunnybrook Farm

The Red Badge of Courage

Robinson Crusoe

The Secret Garden

The Story of King Arthur and His Knights

The Strange Case of Dr. Jekyll and Mr. Hyde